ELLIE'S BAD HAIR DAY

PAVILION
CHILDREN'S

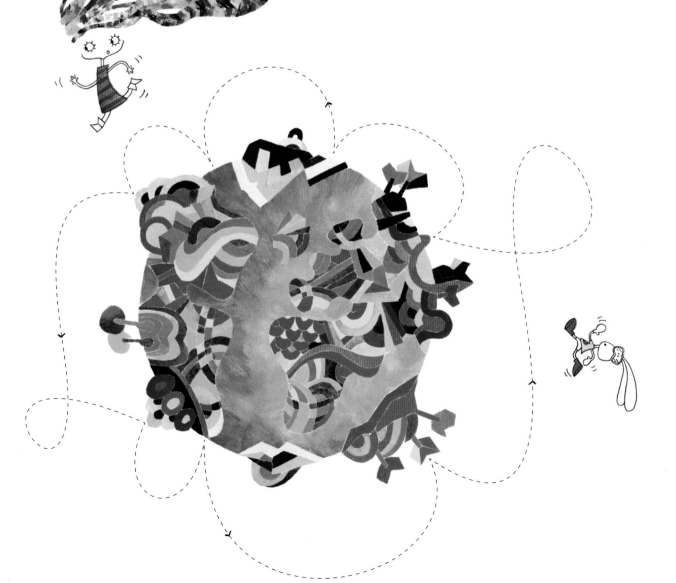

ELLIE&
OSCAR

ELLIE KNOWS WHAT SHE LIKES. AND MORE IMPORTANTLY WHAT SHE DOESN'T.

Things are either
very best or
very worst.

Rarely is anything
very in-the-middle.

Ask Ellie what her
very best is

and you'll always
get the
same reply.

ELLIE

"Easy,
that's Oscar!

He's positively
my absolute best."

And her very worst?
Well that's
easy too.

"MY HAIR IS BAD. IT'S LIKE A TERRIBLE SOMETHING. BUT WORSE. BETWEEN SEVEN OR EIGHT TIMES WORSE."

OSCAR LIKES MOST THINGS.
BUT NOT ALL THE SAME AMOUNT.

Most things are OK, goodish or fine.
Oscar doesn't spend much time worrying.

Most things make him happy.
But one thing makes him happier
than all the rest.

"Probably all the rest
put together," said Oscar.

"ELLIE."

OSCAR

"ELLIE IS GREAT,
JUST REALLY AWESOME."

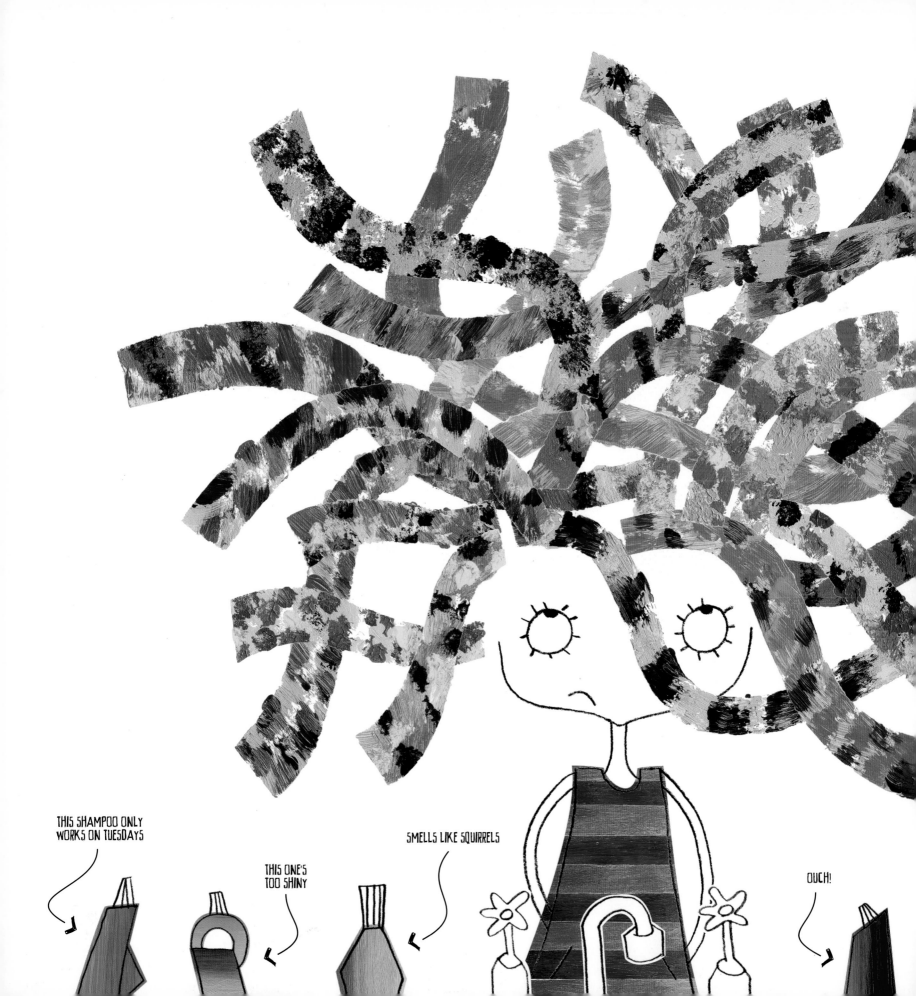

Ellie's hair was wild.

Whatever she wanted it to do, it didn't.
"I've tried every bottle of bubbly,
hair-washing-thing in the house!" said Ellie.

In fact the more time she spent trying
to tame her hair
the worse it got.

Oscar never seemed to
bother with his hair.

He spent exactly
no minutes in the bathroom
every morning.

"Not important," said Oscar.
"It's no big bananas."

"Hmmm! I'm not so sure,"

thought Ellie.

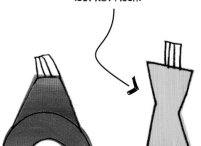

THIS SHAMPOO STRAIGHTENS
(BUT NOT MUCH)

THIS BOTTLE
BENDS THE ENDS

TRIED ONCE.
NEVER AGAIN

TOO YELLOW

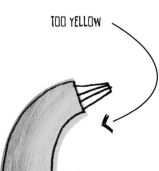

"I'm having a
bad hair day!"

screamed Ellie.

Whatever they tried
her hair just ended
    up looking, well...

...different.

"Not different in a
bad way", thought Oscar,
"but just different."

["A bit like
    broccoli."]

Everybody loved to

"describe"

Ellie's hair.

"It looks a bit like... this",

or

"It looks a bit like... that"
they'd say.

"Reminds me
of that

old cat

we used to have,

who spent all day
asleep
in the washing
machine."

"Remember that

silly bird

who used to live at
the bottom of the garden.
You know, the one who looked
like he had

> too
many
feathers?"

"Not really
very flattering,"
thought Oscar.

Ellie was sad.

ELLIE AND OSCAR'S HOUSE

AROUND THE WORLD
THIS WAY

"**I**'ve had enough!"

said Ellie.

"I'm going to find somebody else like me,
    somebody with hair just like mine."

        Completely ignoring the
    laws of gravity,
    Ellie and Oscar marched down their tree.

        They were going to leave
    their house in the trees and travel
around the world on her scooter.

        "Cool. Let's go crazy!"
                shouted Oscar.

THIS TREE IS TOO SMALL TO LIVE IN

AROUND THE WORLD
THAT WAY ❯

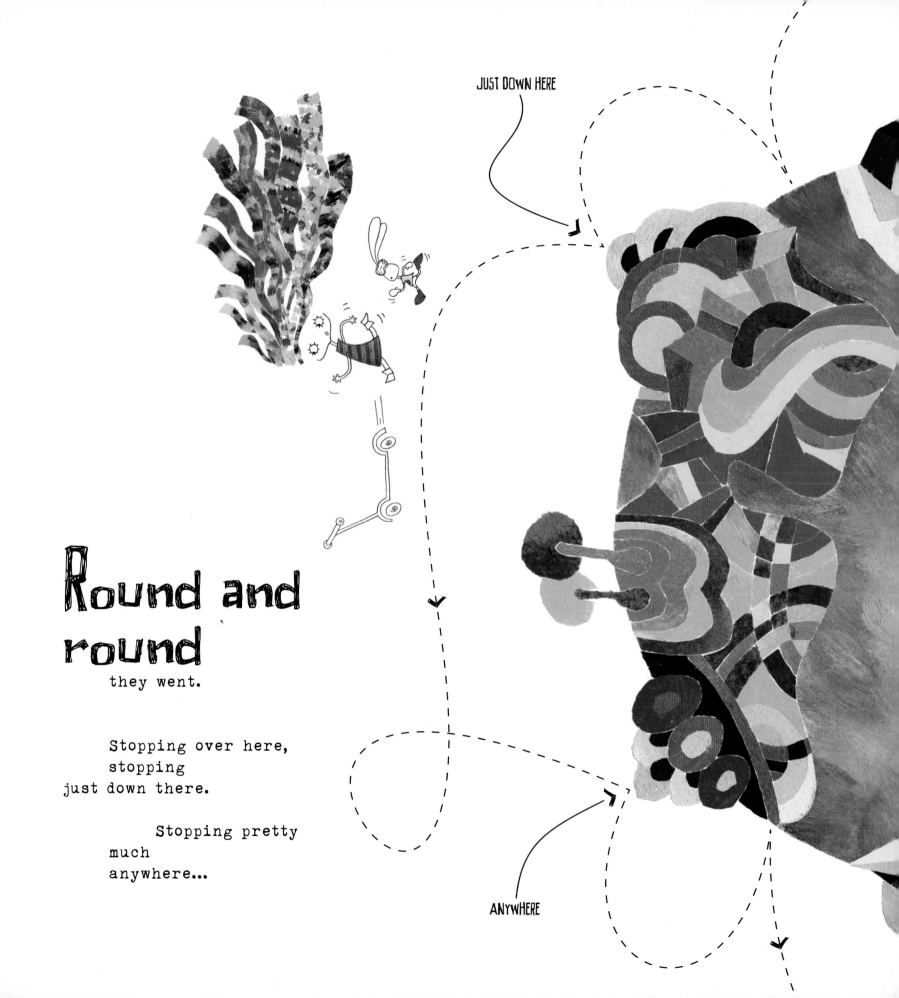

JUST DOWN HERE

Round and round

they went.

Stopping over here,
stopping
just down there.

Stopping pretty
much
anywhere...

ANYWHERE

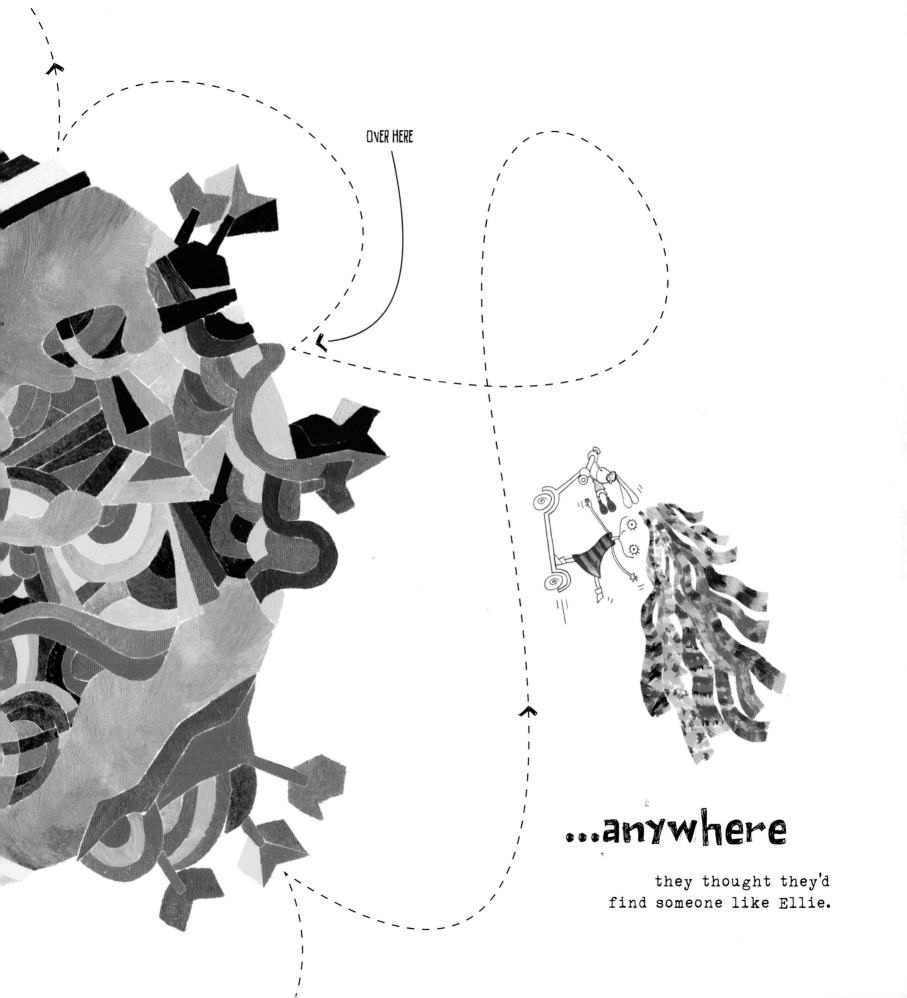

OVER HERE

...anywhere

they thought they'd
find someone like Ellie.

They saw as many
shapes as you
can imagine,

and then some more...

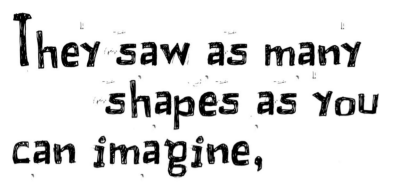

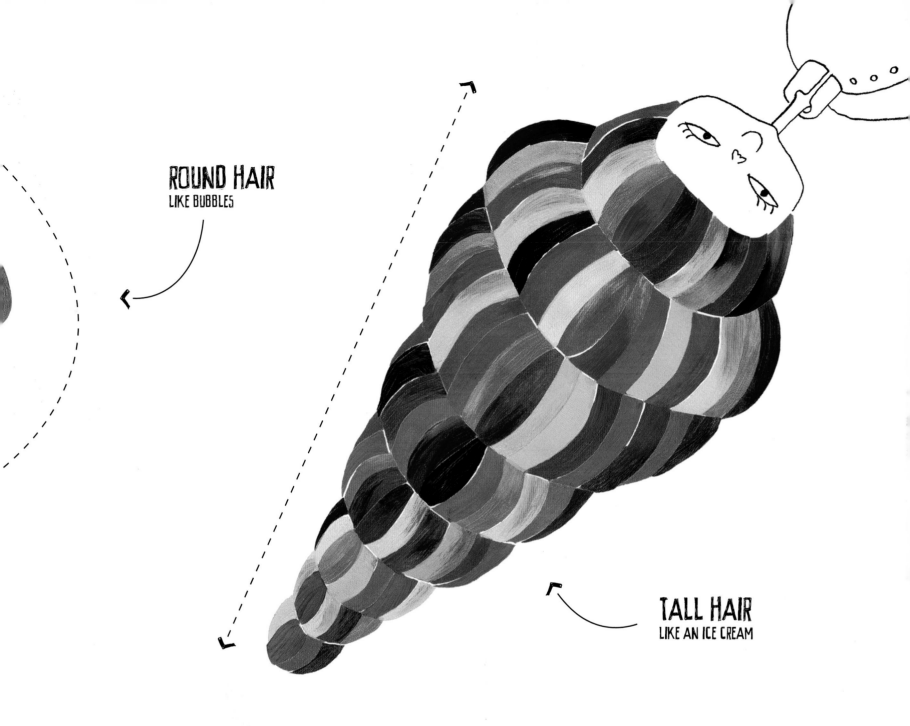

ROUND HAIR
LIKE BUBBLES

TALL HAIR
LIKE AN ICE CREAM

LONG HAIR
LIKE RIBBONS

...But nothing like Ellie.
Similar, but not the same.

Were they ever going to find somebody?

"NOT TOO FAST!"
"NOT TOO FAST!"

shouted Oscar.

Ellie tended to get a bit over enthusiastic on her scooter.

Rushing around, Ellie wasn't looking where they were going or remembering the way back.

Before they knew it they had gone round the world four times.

Oscar started to worry.

If they weren't careful they were going to get...

LOST!

...yes, you guessed it.

As Ellie looked around,
only one thought entered her mind.

**"I haven't the tiniest idea
where we are,"**

she announced.

Oscar agreed.

This didn't look like
anywhere he'd been before.

Back at home her
friends missed her a huge amount
and were all very
busy trying to find her.

But they were having
no luck at all.

"Where's Ellie gone?
Where's all the colour?"

They all wondered.

It was so dull
without her.

LOOKING REALLY HARD

SHOUTING REALLY LOUD

FEELING REALLY SAD

THINKING REALLY HARD

JUST REALLY CONFUSED

Surely there must be a better
way to find her?

Just then, one of
them had an idea.

"What about my...

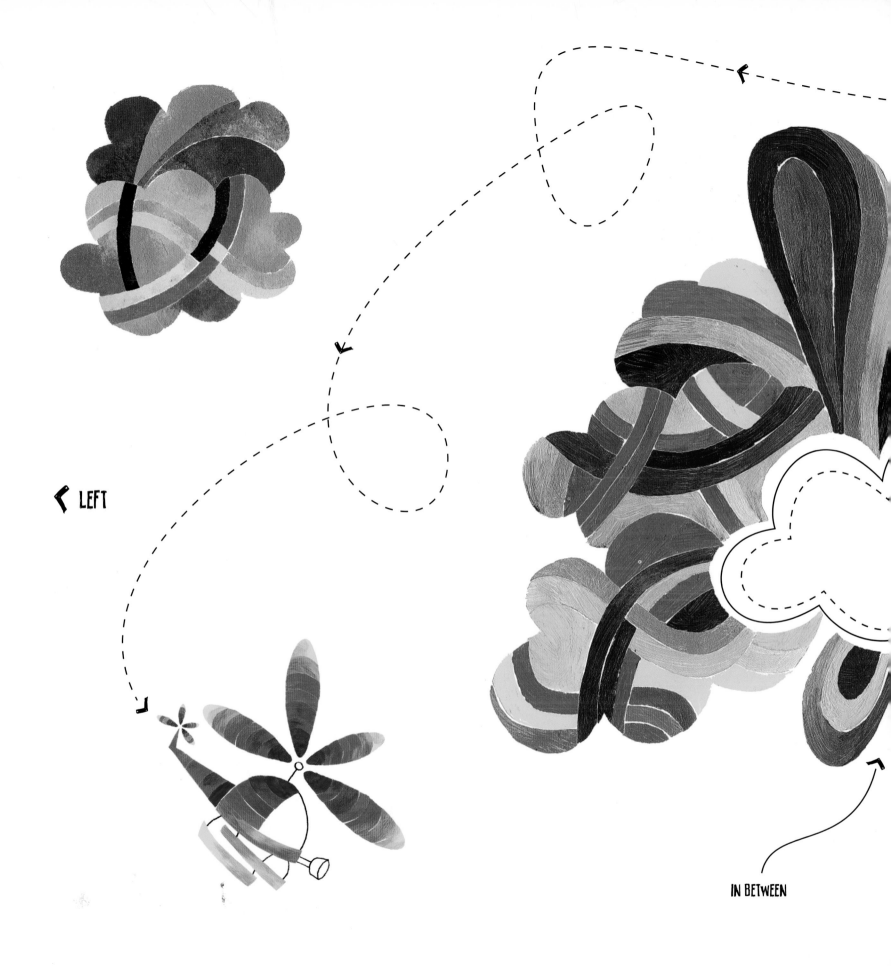

LEFT

IN BETWEEN

UP

JUST BEHIND

... helicopter!"

They all jumped in
and raced off.

They buzzed and zoomed around,
looking everywhere.

They looked up and down,
left and right, back and front.

They even looked in between
and just behind.

RIGHT >

But they couldn't see them.

Many hours passed
and they wondered
if they would ever find them.

But then...

DOWN

...out of the
corner of their eye,
they spotted a small,
bright, colourful spot.

They set the helicopter to

VERY, VERY FAST

and zoomed toward the spot.

As they got closer the
spot got bigger and bigger,
brighter and brighter.

THEY'D
FOUND THEM!

Ellie's hair shone
out like a beacon.

Her hair shone brighter
than anything
else around.

Remember the last time
you were really happy?

So happy it felt like flying?

Well, that's how happy Ellie and Oscar were.

Ellie's friends loved her just the way she was.
Precisely the way she was, to be exact.

"Nothing to change.
Not even the smallest,
tiniest little thing,"
said Oscar.

"DIFFERENT IS GOOD.
AND IT'S GOOD TO BE DIFFERENT,"
shouted Ellie.

"Everybody's different
and that's fun."

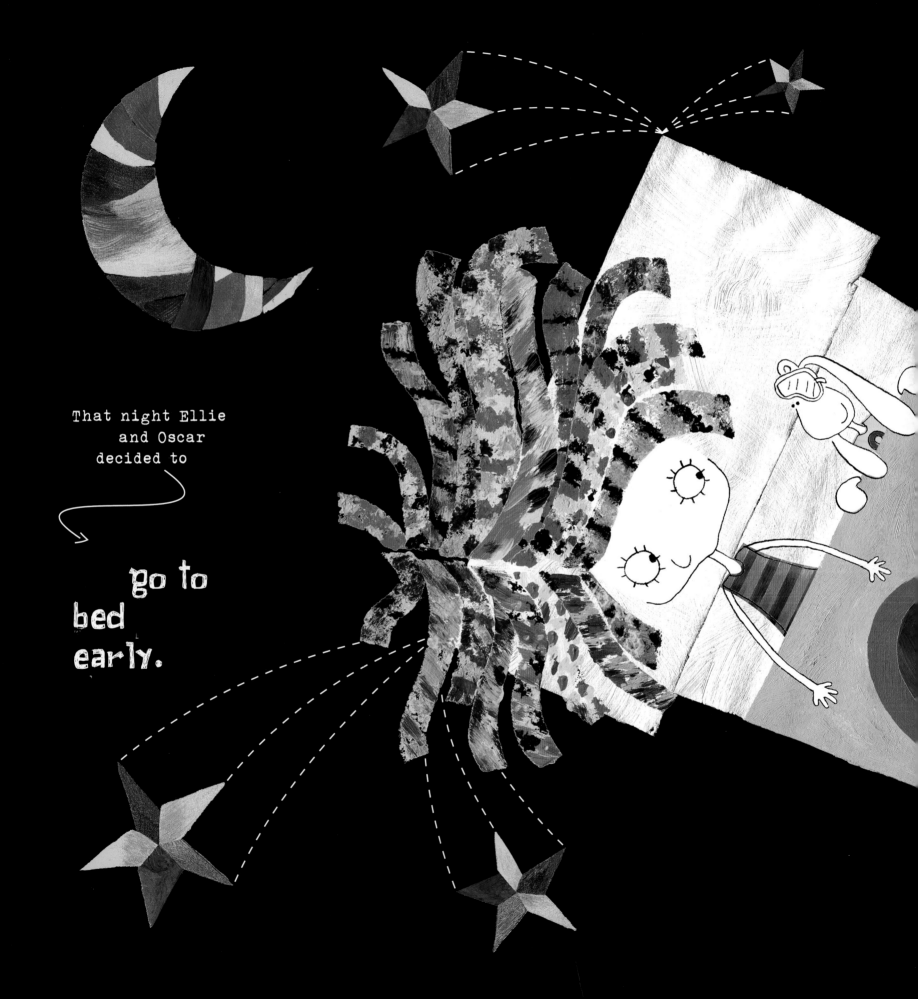

That night Ellie
and Oscar
decided to

go to
bed
early.

Ellie looked at Oscar and
Oscar looked at Ellie. "This has been

a good hair day,"

sighed Ellie.

Oscar agreed.

For the real Ellie.
Love Mama and Papa.

Ellie's Bad Hair Day
        By Jerome Keane
        Illustrated by Susana de Dios

First published in the United Kingdom in 2010 by

Pavilion Children's Books
        10 Southcombe Street
        London
        W14 0RA

An imprint of Anova Books Company Ltd

ISBN: 978-1-84365-140-6

        A CIP catalogue record for this book
is available from the British Library.

10 9 8 7 6 5 4 3 2 1

        Reproduction by Rival Colour Ltd, UK
                Printed and bound by Imago, China
        This book can be ordered direct from the publisher at the
website: www.anovabooks.com, or try your local bookshop.

www.ellieandoscar.com